The Jumblies

The Hills of the Chankly Bore

The Western Sea

A Land All covered in Trees

For Lily I.B.

THE JUMBLIES
A CORGI BOOK 0 552 54690 9

First published in Great Britain by Doubleday,
an imprint of Random House Children's Books

Doubleday edition published 2001
Corgi edition published 2002

1 3 5 7 9 10 8 6 4 2

Copyright © Ian Beck 2001
Designed by Ian Butterworth

Corgi Books are published by Random House Children's Books,
61-63 Uxbridge Road, London W5 5SA,
a division of The Random House Group Ltd,
in Australia by Random House Australia (Pty) Ltd,
20 Alfred Street, Milsons Point, Sydney, NSW 2061, Australia,
in New Zealand by Random House New Zealand Ltd,
18 Poland Road, Glenfield, Auckland 10, New Zealand,
and in South Africa by Random House (Pty) Ltd,
Endulini, 5A Jubilee Road, Parktown 2193, South Africa

THE RANDOM HOUSE GROUP Limited Reg. No. 954009
www.kidsatrandomhouse.co.uk

A CIP catalogue record for this book is available from the British Library.

Printed in Singapore by Tien Wah Press [PTE] Ltd

The Jumblies

Edward Lear

Illustrated by

Ian Beck

PICTURE CORGI BOOKS

They went to sea in a Sieve, they did,

In a Sieve they went to sea;

In spite of all their friends could say,

On a winter's morn, on a stormy day,

In a Sieve they went to sea!

And when the Sieve turned round and round,

And everyone cried, "You'll all be drowned!"

They called aloud, "Our Sieve ain't big,

But we don't care a button! We don't care a fig!

In a Sieve we'll go to sea!"

But we don't care a button!

We don't care a fig!

Far and few, far and few,
Are the lands where the Jumblies live;
Their heads are green, and their hands are blue,
And they went to sea in a Sieve.

They sailed away in a Sieve, they did,
    In a Sieve they sailed so fast,
With only a beautiful pea-green veil
    Tied with a riband by way of a sail,
To a small tobacco-pipe mast;

And everyone said, who saw them go,

"O won't they be soon upset, you know!

For the sky is dark, and the voyage is long,

And happen what may, it's extremely wrong

In a Sieve to sail so fast!"

O won't they be
soon upset, you know!

For the sky is dark,
and the voyage is long

Far and Few, Far and Few,
Are the lands where the Jumblies live;
Their heads are green, and their hands are blue,
And they went to sea in a Sieve.

The water it soon came in, it did,

The water it soon came in;

So to keep them dry, they wrapped their feet

In a pinky paper all folded neat,

And they fastened it down with a pin.

And they passed the night in a crockery-jar,

And each of them said, "How wise we are!

Though the sky be dark, and the voyage be long,

Yet we never can think we were rash or wrong,

While round in our Sieve we spin!"

How wise we are!

Far and Few, Far and Few,
Are the lands where the Jumblies live;
Their heads are green, and their hands are blue,
And they went to sea in a Sieve.

And all night long they sailed away;
And when the sun went down,
They whistled and warbled a moony song
To the echoing sound of a coppery gong,
In the shade of the mountains brown.

"O Timballo! How happy we are,

When we live in a Sieve and a crockery-jar,

And all night long in the moonlight pale,

We sail away with a pea-green sail,

In the shade of the mountains brown!"

O Timballo!
How happy
we are

Far and few, far and few,
Are the lands where the Jumblies live;
Their heads are green, and their hands are blue,
And they went to sea in a Sieve.

They sailed to the Western Sea, they did,
   To a land all covered with trees,
And they bought an Owl, and a useful Cart,
   And a pound of Rice, and a Cranberry Tart,
And a hive of silvery Bees.

And they bought a Pig, and some green Jack-daws,

And a lovely Monkey with lollipop paws,

And forty bottles of Ring-Bo-Ree,

And no end of Stilton Cheese.

Far and few, far and few,
Are the lands where the Jumblies live;
Their heads are green, and their hands are blue,
And they went to sea in a Sieve.

And in twenty years they all came back,

In twenty years or more,

And everyone said, "How tall they've grown!

For they've been to the Lakes, and the Torrible Zone,

And the hills of the Chankly Bore";

And they drank their health, and gave them a feast
Of dumplings made of beautiful yeast;
And everyone said, "If we only live,
We too will go to sea in a Sieve,
To the hills of the Chankly Bore!"

Far and Few, Far and Few,
Are the lands where the Jumblies live;
Their heads are green, and their hands are blue,
And they went to sea in a Sieve.

We too will go to sea in a Sieve...

The Hills of the Chankly Bore

The Western Sea

A Land All Covered in Trees

The Torrible Zone